We Are the Hocky Family

I am Mr. Hocky!

I am Mrs. Hocky!

I am Baby Hocky!

I am Henry Hocky!

I am Holly Hocky!

I am Newton!

Balloon Story

I have a balloon.
Do you have a balloon?
I have a balloon.

The Happy Hocky Family

!

Lane Smith

VIKING

FOR
Dr. Mary Leach

FOR
Bert Leach

—L.S.

My balloon is red.
If you had a balloon,
what color would it be?

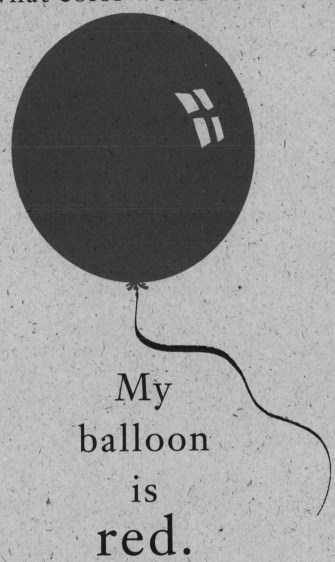

My
balloon
is
red.

POP!

10

I have a string.

Do you have a string?

I have a string.

Holly's Boat

Holly's boat will not float.
"Little boat, why won't you float?"
asks Holly.
"Do not be afraid, little boat.
You can do it...FLOAT!"

"You're right!" said Holly's boat.
"I CAN do it..."

"I CAN DO IT..."

Holly's boat floated away and away.

Holly had to buy a new boat.

Henry's Birthday

HOORAY!

Today is Henry's birthday.

LOOK,

Henry has made a list
of the presents he wants.

For my 7th Birthday
I want:

- A new set of crayons.

- An electric car.

- A black and white
pony with a
silver saddle.

WHEW!

Today is the day after Henry's birthday.

LOOK,

Henry has made a list of the
presents he wants next year.

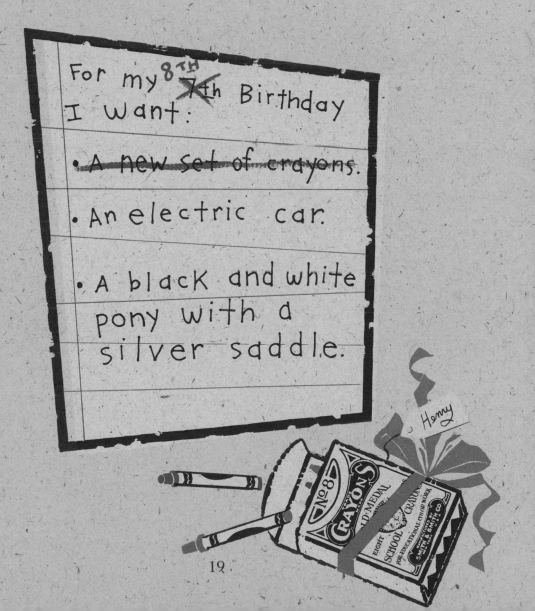

For my 8TH ~~7th~~ Birthday
I want:

- ~~A new set of crayons.~~

- An electric car.

- A black and white
  pony with a
  silver saddle.

Chores: Quiz #1

Today was Holly's day to do the laundry.
See if you can match the pocket items
before and after the dryer.

BEFORE

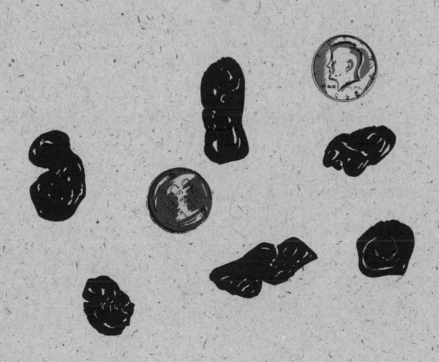

AFTER

Chores: Quiz #2

Today was
Henry's day
to do the dishes.
Can you guess
how many dishes
this many pieces make?

Ant Farm

I like to study nature.

I have an
ant
farm.

These ants are my RESPONSIBILITY.

"RESPONSIBILITY"

is a big word. It means my ants
count on me to take care of them.

For example, today is a very hot day.

My ants have no windows to open.

How can I help?

It is my responsibility.

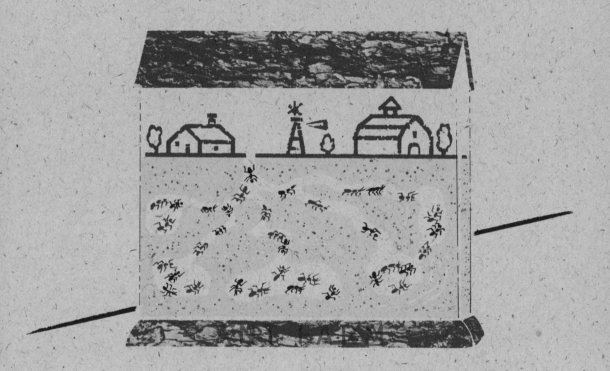

I know how!

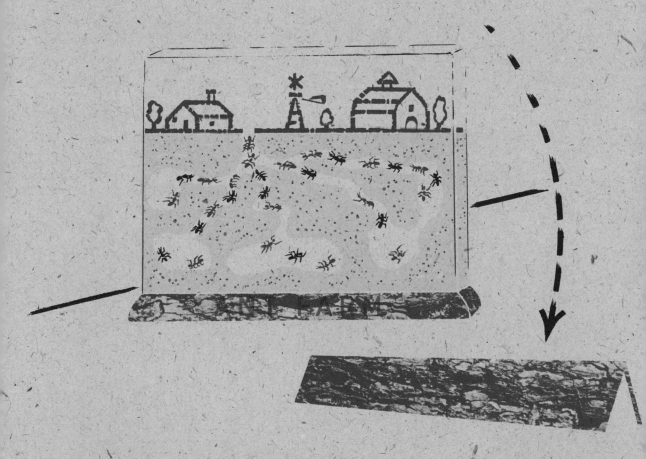

My ants count on me to take care of them.

New Kitchen

Mr. and Mrs. Hocky have
remodeled their kitchen.

See the white cabinets.
See the shiny counters.
See the shelves for spices
and cereal and sugar.

Pretty kitchen.
New kitchen.
Clean kitchen.

Coat Story

I have a white coat.
Do you have a white coat?
I have a white coat.

I have a SNOWY white coat.

I have a sno—

S P L A S H

I have a white hat.
Do you have a white hat?

I have a white hat.

Grandma Hocky

Grandma has come to visit.
Grandma's perfume
smells like flowers.

LOTS
and
LOTS
of
FLOWERS

"Grandma,
do you hear
the Magic Monkey?
He is calling
us from outside!

Open the window so we can
hear him, Grandma.

OPEN

the

WINDOW

WIDE!"

Toys

We like our toys.
We take CARE of our TOYS.
We do not want
our toys to become broken.

We want to keep our toys
for a long time.

Cousin Stinky has
come over to play.

"Where are your toys?"
he asks.

"What is 'TOYS'?" we ask.
"We do not know
what that word means."

Cousin Stinky has left.

We like our toys.

Henry's Airplanes

I am making paper airplanes.
SEE the AIRPLANES fly!

FLY! FLY! FLY!

Holly has come into the room.
She is upset.
She can't find her homework.

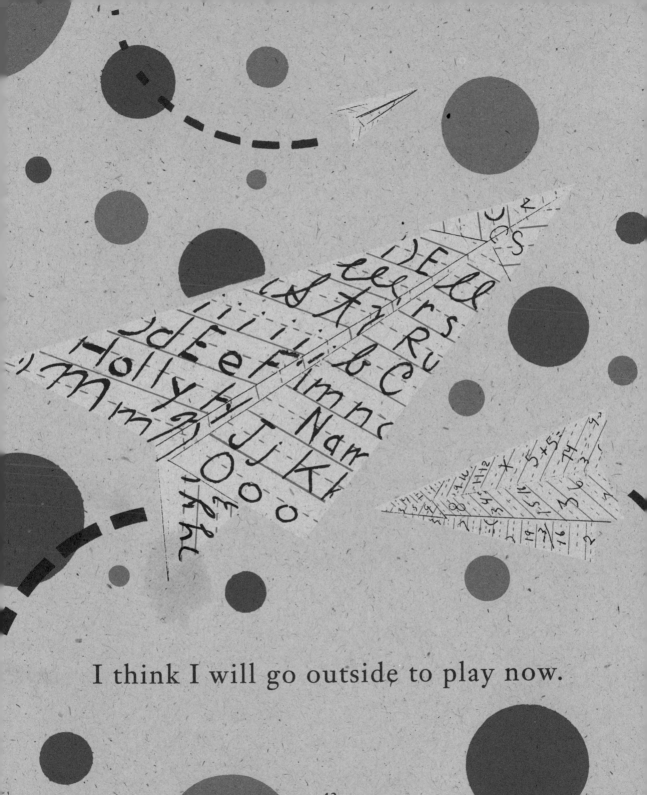

I think I will go outside to play now.

Holly's Lullaby

Henry is taking his nap.

Poor Henry.

He is very tired.

He is tired from chasing me

around all day with a dead spider.

Poor Henry.

Nap time is good.

Nap time is good for Henry.

Nap time is good for dollies too.
My dolly needs a nap.
I will play my dolly a lullaby
to help her sleep.

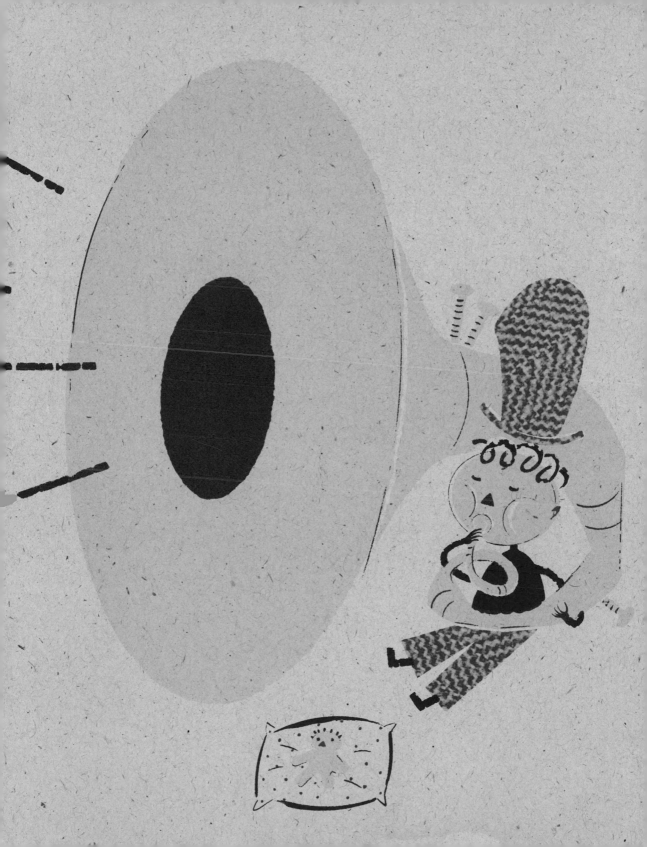

Skateboard

We do not
skate
down the
hill.
We
do not
like
BROKEN
BONES.
We
always
play
SAFE.

What
does not
have
bones
to break?
Dollies
do not
have
bones.
LUCKY
DOLLY.

The Zoo

The Hockys are at the zoo.

"I like the birds!" says Mr. Hocky.

"I like the monkeys!" says Mrs. Hocky.

"I like the fish!" says Henry Hocky.

"I like the deer!" says Holly Hocky.

"I like the seals!" says Baby Hocky.

"I like the crocodiles!" says Newton.

The Hockys are home from the zoo.
"I liked the birds!" says Mr. Hocky.
"I liked the monkeys!" says Mrs. Hocky.
"I liked the fish!" says Henry Hocky.
"I liked the deer!" says Holly Hocky.
"I liked the seals!" says Baby Hocky.

Henry's Bedtime Story

"Holly,
do you know the story
of the
MONSTER
who comes to
STEAL
little children
in the night?

"He comes into kids' bedrooms
at twelve midnight.

Big MONSTER.
Scary MONSTER.
Bad MONSTER."

"I will lock the door after you leave,"
said Holly.
"You don't have to worry about that,
silly,...

...the Monster only comes in
through windows."

Candy Apple Story

I have a candy apple.
Do you have a candy apple?
I have a candy apple.

My candy apple is crunchy.
Is your candy apple crunchy?

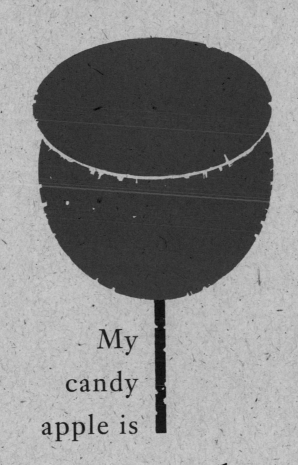

My
candy
apple is

crunchy.

CRACK!

I have a tooth for the Tooth Fairy.
Do you have a tooth for
the Tooth Fairy?
I have a tooth for the Tooth Fairy.

Good-bye

Cousin Stinky and the Stinky family
have come to visit.
Mr. Stinky has his box of vacation slides.
Mrs. Stinky is holding a fruitcake.
It is time to turn out all the lights.
It is time to say good-bye.
Good-bye from the Hocky family.

 KNOCK!

KNOCK!

"Good-bye...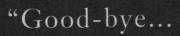

Shhhhhhh..."